Also by James Preller

I Scream, You Scream!

JAMES PRELLER

SCARY TALES

HOME SWEET HORROR

Illustrated by IACOPO BRUNO

MACMILLAN CHILDREN'S BOOKS

First published in the US 2013 by Feiwel and Friends

This edition published 2013 by Macmillan Children's Books
a division of Macmillan Publishers Limited
20 New Wharf Road, London N1 9RR
Basingstoke and Oxford
Associated companies throughout the world
www.panmacmillan.com

ISBN 978-1-4472-4683-1

3 5 7 9 8 6 4 2

A CIP catalogue record for this book is available from
the British Library.

Book design by Ashley Halsey
Printed and bound by CPI Group (UK) Ltd, Croydon CR0 4YY

*This book is dedicated to Maggie Preller,
my favorite terror, who first told me
about Bloody Mary.*

CONTENTS

BLOODY MARY

BLOODY MARY

BLOODY MARY

WELCOME TO THE NEW HOME OF THE FINN FAMILY. DON'T BE AFRAID. WIPE YOUR FEET ON THE MAT. AH.

HOME SWEET HORROR

COME, STEP INSIDE. BUT BE WARNED. THIS OLD HOUSE ONLY SEEMS EMPTY. BECAUSE THANKS TO A HARMLESS CHILDREN'S GAME, BLOODY MARY JUST MIGHT MAKE AN APPEARANCE IN A MIRROR NEAR YOU.

CAREFUL NOW. SHE SCRATCHES. SEE, THERE'S BLOOD UNDER HER FINGER-NAILS.

ANY QUESTIONS, JUST ASK. BECAUSE THIS OLD HOUSE IS DYING TO TALK.

THE HOUSE
ON THE HILL

'Wake up, Liam. We're here,' Mr Finn whispered from the driver's seat. 'Our new home.'

The eight-year-old boy rubbed his eyes, groggy from the long drive. He looked out the car window, blinking into the dark. 'What time is it?'

'Around midnight,' his father said. 'You three have been crashed out for hours.'

Liam became aware of the warm body

pressed against him. His hand fell on the sleeping dog's neck. On the other side of the dog, Liam's older sister, Kelly, slept with her head pitched forward. Even in sleep, Kelly's hand clutched her necklace. It was once her mother's ring, a parting gift that Kelly wore on a chain around her neck.

'Let her rest,' Mr Finn said, as if reading Liam's mind. 'I've been enjoying the peace and quiet.'

Kelly had been against the move. She'd crossed her arms and vowed, 'Nuh-uh, I'm not going. I like it here in Hopeville.' She'd argued, thrown tantrums, said horrible things. But Mr Finn decided that it was time for a fresh start, and that was that. Their mother would have wanted it this way.

Liam felt his chest tighten at the thought. Even after nearly two years, her memory caused his heart to swell and his breath to grow short and shallow, like the early signs of an asthma attack. He fingered the inhaler in his pocket. *Breathe in, breathe out,* he told himself. *Breathe in, breathe out.*

The road was quiet, with dim streetlights and a few darkened homes across the way. Each house was set apart on high, rolling lots, not as crowded as Liam's old neighbourhood. He looked back at the battered old house on the hill. It was big, larger than he'd imagined from the photographs. The two windows on the second floor – with half-drawn shades like lazy yellow eyelids – reminded Liam of watchful eyes. He imagined that the house looked down upon them out of those eyes. Looming, waiting, watching. The front door's brass knocker looked like a nose.

The dog, Doolin, rose stiffly on ancient legs. She stretched, sniffed, and whined softly in the dark of night.

'What's the matter, girl? You need to do your business?'

Liam opened the door. He stepped into a bath of warm, late-summer air. He beckoned to the dog. 'Come on, girl. Let's check out the new place,' Liam urged.

The dog did not budge. Instead, she backed away, pressing into Kelly.

Liam's sister stirred, grumbled. 'Shut up, Liam, will ya? I'm trying to sleep.'

She pushed the dog away.

Mr Finn unlocked the boot, moved around to the back of the car. The big removal van with all their belongings would be arriving tomorrow. 'Don't expect a palace,' Mr Finn called out brightly. He pulled out three sleeping bags, pillows, a torch. 'It'll be fun, like a camping trip. Just remember, guys. This place needs a lot of work.'

A flicker of light caught Liam's eye. He

glanced up at the house. And a zip of fear ran down his spine. Just darkness, silence, and an empty road. *It was nothing*, he told himself. But the sudden flash appeared again, a flicker of light from one of the windows. On, then

off. Liam glanced at his father. Mr Finn didn't see it.

The light came from the window on the right. *Maybe my bedroom*, Liam guessed. It felt to Liam as if the house's great eye had opened and shut. A wink. As if to say, *I know a secret*.

'There's no one inside?' Liam asked.

'Don't be a dweeb,' Kelly grumbled. She climbed out of the car, unfolding her long limbs. 'I seriously doubt that anybody besides us would live in a dump like this.'

Liam ignored Kelly's comment. The death of their mother had changed his sister. Nowadays, she seemed angry all the time. Liam missed his sister, the good times they used to share. These days she shut herself off, spending hours alone in her room. Maybe things would get better in the new place.

Ed Finn put a strong arm around his son's

shoulders. 'This old house has been empty for two years,' he said. 'It's a work-in-progress. That's why I got such a great price.'

A MOAN,
A WHISPER

From the first day, Liam heard noises. The groan of floorboards. The hiss of radiators. The clatter of wind pounding the shutters.

CREAK and **SCREECH, RASP** and **WHEEZE** and **BANG**.

And Liam sometimes thought he heard a muffled voice. A moan, a whispered something that caused him to turn up the television, loud.

His dad said it was the typical noises that come with an old, unfamiliar house. 'You'll get used to it,' he told Liam. 'It's what gives the place – I don't know – *character*. Yeah, that's the word. Character.'

Liam didn't see it that way. He sensed that the house was trying to speak. As if it had something to say. A message. But who could he tell? No one would believe him. 'Liam and his overactive imagination,' they'd explain. He was, everyone said, a dreamy boy. Still, Liam was unable to make out the exact message. What was the house trying to tell him? Who else had lived in this place, moving like shadows through the walls?

Who had lived here before?

WHAM.

A door slammed shut.

'Dad? Kelly?'

No answer. Kelly was outside, her long hair pulled back in an athletic ponytail, throwing a basketball at a rusted rim in the driveway. He could hear Kelly dribbling on the cement, hear as the ball rattled against the backboard. An engine's dull hum told Liam that Mr Finn was riding the mower over the lawn. Cutting the grass, trying to tame the shaggy yard.

Liam was alone in the house.

Next Liam heard . . . water? He moved cautiously towards the hallway bathroom, the one he shared with his sister. He put his ear to the door. The shower was running.

Liam knocked. No answer. He called out, 'Kelly?' No answer came. He scratched roughly at his red, uncombed hair and made a decision. He turned the knob, gently pushed open the door. The room was filled with smoke. No, not smoke. Steam. So thick it was impossible to see. Liam reached into the empty shower stall, shut off the hot water.

The mirror was fogged up. As the steam leaked out through the open door, the mirror returned to normal. Clean and clear – except for a few cloudy lines. At first, Liam didn't understand what he was seeing. Because the letters in the mirror were reversed.

The message read:

Mine? Liam gasped.

Another door opened somewhere. Liam poked his head around the corner, looked downstairs. It was his father. Mr Finn wiped his hands on his jeans, stomped his work boots. Liam followed his father into the kitchen. The big man stood, one hand leaning on the counter, listening to his mobile with a frown on his face.

He shook his head, hung up.

'Who was that?' Liam asked.

'I don't get it.' Mr Finn looked at Liam. 'Doesn't anybody want to work in this town? That's the third carpenter who's turned me down cold.'

'Maybe you don't pay enough,' Liam joked.

'I pay plenty,' Mr Finn grumbled. 'It's just these local guys . . . I don't know what's wrong with 'em.' Mr Finn pulled some sausage and a loaf of white bread from the fridge. 'You hungry?'

Liam said he was.

He wanted to tell his father how it felt the very first time he stepped into the house. That shivery feeling. A sense that something wasn't right. But not today. His father was too stressed already. He had a new job at the factory, a new house, two kids to worry about, and no wife.

Liam decided to keep his fears to himself.

NOISES IN THE
BASEMENT

Liam stood in the hallway off the kitchen, peering into the basement. The stairs were ancient wooden boards nailed across empty space. One false step and it was a long drop to the cement floor below. The basement gave off a smell of decay, of things gone rotten. A place where mice had crawled off to die. Home to cobwebs and spiders, trapped flies and ruined toys.

Liam flicked the switch on the wall. Nothing happened.

At the bottom of the stairs, he could scarcely make out the bare bulb that hung from the ceiling. It had a pull string. Maybe that would do the trick.

But an inner voice made Liam cautious. He remembered his father's warning during breakfast. 'I'll be gone most of the day,' he said. 'I know you like to explore, Liam. And that's fine. Up to a point. But stay out of the attic, and don't go into the basement. I don't trust those old stairs. And that old furnace needs to be replaced. It's an accident waiting to happen.'

When Liam stepped back to shut the basement door, a metallic sound came to his ears.

CLANG

CLANG

CLANG.

The sound came from . . . *down there*.

'Hello?' he bleated.

Again, in a stronger voice, 'Anybody down there?'

Liam wiped his hands on his trousers. He looked around. Puffed on his inhaler and thought about things. *Breathe in, breathe out*. Kelly was upstairs in her room. Still asleep, most likely. Or texting, texting, texting – like always. His father away on errands: groceries, the timber yard, who knows where?

All Liam really knew was that he was alone.

In the house.

Or alone *with* the house.

CLANG, CLANG.
CLANG-CLANG-CLANG.

The sounds echoed up in rhythm, like a voice

calling to him, a song in the dark.

Come, Liam. Come.

Doolin stood protectively at Liam's side. **GRRRR**, she growled. A warning sound, low, from deep inside the animal's chest. **GRRRR**, **GRRRR**.

The metallic noises came louder now, more urgent. Clearer. They were calling to Liam. *Come, come.*

Transfixed, Liam took one cautious step down the stairs. There was no railing, nothing to grip. He shifted his weight from his left foot to his right. There, **CREAK**, the old board held strong. Some fluttery something brushed across Liam's face, like the shadowy hand of a ghost.

No, it was only a cobweb, a spider's trap.

'Come on, girl,' Liam called to his dog. 'Let's explore together.'

The dog sank to the floor, head on her

paws. She growled, a rolling rumble of fear and warning.

'What's the matter? Too dark for you?' Liam asked, honey in his voice. 'You've never been bothered by stairs before.'

The dog whined.

'Come,' Liam ordered, his voice deeper. The sound of command.

Doolin inched away.

Liam shrugged, moved down another step, and another. Halfway down, he could bend at the waist to peer into the vast, dank basement. It was filled with crowded shelves, boxes, and broken furniture.

CLANG, CLANG, CLANG,

banged the noises. It was something in the far back corner, a heavy, black shape. The furnace, perhaps. That was the source of the sounds. At last Liam reached the lightbulb, pulled on the string. There was a burst of wild electrical light and – *POP!* – the bare bulb shattered into pieces.

It startled Liam. He sensed a shape drifting through the basement, soundless and black, moving towards him. He turned and ran up the stairs, taking them two at a time, landing heavily with each step. **CRASH!** a board cracked and Liam fell, slamming his shin hard against the wood. He grabbed the top step, catching himself before he fell. He wheezed, felt dizzy, woozy. Liam's left leg dangled in the air, kicking at nothingness. He felt a thin, skeletal grip around his ankle. Like a claw pulling, dragging him down. Liam yanked his leg free, lifted himself up, gasping for air, and scrambled to the top of the stairs. He crawled into the kitchen, into the light. He slammed the door shut behind him and twisted the lock, heart thundering

BOOM-BOOM,
BOOM-BOOM,
BOOM-BOOM.

His back against the door, Liam sat on the floor, legs splayed. He took a puff from his inhaler. And another. *Breathe in*, he reminded himself. *Breathe out*.

Breathe in, breathe out.

Down below, through the door, he swore he heard the sound . . . of laughter.

A STRANGER'S WARNING

An hour later, Kelly came down and planted herself on the living-room couch. Her nose was in a book, a tender love story about killer zombies.

'Do you think there's anything creepy about this house?' Liam asked.

Kelly rolled her eyes. 'Creepy? Yeah, you.'

'Come on, Kelly. You know what I mean.'

Kelly put down the book. 'There's lots of things that are creepy about this house, Liam.

Everything is so old and musty and gross. Even the phone is like a million years old. A dial phone? Really? What's up with that?'

'Dad says it's a work-in-progress,' Liam countered.

'Ha!' Kelly scoffed.

'Can a house be . . . alive?' Liam ventured. 'Like with, I don't know, a spirit or something?'

'Oh, please, just shoot me now,' Kelly groaned. She turned her attention back to the book.

The phone rang.

And rang.

'Get it,' Kelly snapped.

'I'm not your slave. You answer it,' Liam replied.

No one moved.

After the fifth ring, the answer machine picked up.

A man's voice spoke. 'Hello, Mr Finn, this

is Harry Christiansen. You called about some repair work. Look, I don't know how to say this except . . . you really need to get out of that house. It's a bad place, pure evil. Nothing good can come of it. Just take your kids and don't look back. I mean, thanks for the call. I really do appreciate the offer for work in these tough times. But please, don't call back.'

CLICK.

He hung up.

Kelly closed the book. She stared at Liam, a question in her eyes. They played the message over again.

'What a creepster,' Kelly concluded.

'You don't believe him?' Liam asked.

Kelly shrugged.

'I just wonder,' Liam said.

'Yeah?' Kelly asked.

'Like, who lived here before us?' Liam said. 'And what happened to them?'

5

THE NIGHT MESSAGE

Liam lay on his bed, the blankets tossed aside except for one thin sheet. The night air was sweltering. Liam felt like bread warming in a toaster. He rose to plug an old fan they'd found in the closet into the wall socket. It made a horrible clatter – loose screws and rattling metal. Liam unplugged it. No way could he sleep through that racket.

He collapsed back into bed. Liam turned

over his pillow again and again, searching hopelessly for a cool side.

He thought of his mother. She'd been gone for almost two years. Liam was in first grade when she died. At the time, he felt so lost and confused. Kelly reacted differently. She got mad – angry that her mother left, angry over the long illness. And though Liam's father tried his best, he grew withdrawn. On many mornings, Liam found his father sitting at the breakfast nook, food uneaten, staring into space.

Everyone crawled into their own shells. And burrowed deep, like turtles in mud.

It had been a long, sad year – but eventually Mr Finn emerged from his gloom, like a new bud shooting forth after a cold, hard winter. 'We're moving to Upstate New York,' he announced one night. 'I got an offer for a job as a foreman in a new chemical plant.

They promise better hours, more pay. It's too good to pass up.'

And so here they were. Somewhere in the grey middle of nowhere, called Upstate New York.

Liam shifted in his bed, stared out the bedroom window into the night sky. It was crowded with stars. Little pinpricks of wonder, lit at an impossible distance from home.

I wish I may, I wish I might. His lips moved soundlessly.

Liam drifted off to sleep.

He half awoke, groggy at first, to the sensation of cool air across his face. He lifted his head and saw the fan's blades, rotating in a blur. But something was different. What was it? Silence. The old fan worked noiselessly.

Had his father turned it on while he slept?

Then the noises started, ever so faintly, like a quivering whisper. Like a voice from far away. **Wwwaaan,** it trembled. **Waaaannnnchu. Waaaantt . . . chuuu.**

The words pulsed from the fan. It was trying to speak, Liam was sure of it. **'Want you . . . want you . . . gooooone.'**

Gone.

Want you gone.

Liam leaped out of bed. The fan moved slowly, like a head swivelling from side to side, repeating '**GOOONE, GOOONE, GOOONE**,' over and over in vibrating, eerie tones.

Liam moved to flick the switch to OFF. But it was already set to that position. Liam next tried to pull the plug out of the wall socket.

But it was resting on the rug.

Already unplugged.

Yet the fan churned ceaselessly on.

'**WANT YOU GONE**,' it said. Over and over again.

'Shut up,' Liam cried. 'Shut up!'

Mr Finn never got the full story. The next morning, he found the old fan in the garbage on the side of the house.

'How'd this get here?' he wondered. 'Liam, you know?'

Liam shrugged, looked away. 'Beats me,' he replied.

BLOODY MARY

Kelly's best friend in the world, Mitali Dristi, finally came for a weekend visit. It was, for Kelly, the biggest deal in the world. It turned out that Mitali had relatives nearby, so after a period of negotiation it was decided that a reunion of the two friends would be possible. Mitali was to be dropped off on a Saturday and picked up the next afternoon. Liam didn't mind. It was nice to see someone from the old neighbourhood, even if it had to be Kelly's most annoying friend.

Mitali's skin was the colour of milk chocolate. She was an athlete, strong and beautiful, with large brown eyes and black hair. She was also a little bossy.

Liam listened from his room as the two girls giggled in the hallway.

'OK, OK, stop pushing. I'll do it,' Kelly said.

'We'll need two candles,' Mitali said. 'And a lighter.'

'Liam!' Kelly called. 'Do you know where Dad keeps the lighter for the grill?'

Liam opened his door. 'It's in the junk drawer by the sink.'

'Well?'

'Well, what?' he asked.

'Get it,' Kelly demanded.

'Why should I?' Liam crossed his arms.

Mitali raised her hands, curving her fingers like wicked claws. 'Because, my dearie, we're going to pay a visit to Bloody Mary!'

'Who's that?' he asked.

'It's a ghost story. Go get the lighter,' Kelly said, bargaining, 'and we'll let you hang around. Just don't let Dad see you.'

Liam shuffled down the stairs, murmuring as he walked:

'Mary, Mary, quite contrary,
How does your garden grow?
With silver bells and cockleshells,
And pretty maids all in a row.'

Liam wondered what made that old rhyme pop into his head. 'Silver bells and cockleshells,' he hummed to himself. He imagined a garden of beautiful flowers.

Liam's father was busy painting the living room. The place looked like a disaster area, with furniture pushed to the middle, empty beer bottles, half-empty cartons of Chinese takeaway, and dust sheets scattered across the floor. Mr Finn had earbuds stuffed into his skull. 'Hi, Dad!' Liam shouted.

'Oh, hey, sport,' Mr Finn said. He waved without looking back, kept right on rolling the paint on to the wall.

'Looks good,' Liam said.

'What?' Mr Finn shouted. He twisted his head to look at Liam.

The boy pointed and gave a thumbs-up.

'Glad you approve,' Mr Finn shouted above the music from his iPod. 'Everything OK?'

'Yeah, Mitali wants us to talk to a ghost,' Liam told his father.

Mr Finn pointed to his ear and shook his head. 'Whatever!'

Liam returned upstairs with the lighter.

They crowded inside the bathroom. Mitali lit the candles and placed one on each side of the sink.

She turned to Kelly. 'Does he really have to be here?'

Kelly looked at freckle-faced Liam. His hair a mess, as always. 'He's OK,' she decided.

'Shut the lights,' Mitali whispered.

The room went dark, except for two flickering candles and the shadows that swayed on the walls.

Mitali placed her hands on Kelly's shoulders. 'Ready?'

Kelly nodded yes.

'Remember, each time you turn, you say "Bloody Mary" and look into the mirror. Your voice should get louder each time.'

'Got it,' Kelly said. And so slowly, slowly she turned, round and round.

Liam stared at the mirror. Mitali counted

out the turns, her lips quivering with excitement. A cold feeling of dread gripped Liam. He wanted to end this game, pull his sister into his arms, cry out, 'Stop!'

But the words never reached his lips.

'BLOODY MARY. BLOODY MARY. BLOODY MARY. BLOODY MARY. BLOODY MARY. BLOODY MARY. BLOODY MARY. BLOODY MARY. BLOODY MARY. BLOODY MARY. BLOODY MARY. BLOODY MARY.'

Kelly began in a whisper, softly and gently, until now, finally, on the thirteenth turn, she bellowed in a thundering shout,

BLOODY MARY!

BREATHE IN, BREATHE OUT . . . NOW SCREAM

They stared in the mirror. Nothing changed.

Liam sighed with relief.

Breathe in, breathe out.

All was calm, all was clear.

And then the candles began to flicker, as if blown by swirling wind. The flames guttered and failed, and the light in the room died with it. The children were plunged into darkness, relieved only by the waxing moon outside the window. And now a fiery glow came from the mirror, as if lit from within.

A shape formed in the glass, a shadowy figure, an ancient face.

Bloody Mary, Liam thought.

Her hair was blood-red and hung loose and shabby around her thin shoulders. A sharp nose and chin gave her face a V shape. And her eyes glowed like flames.

Kelly stood trembling. Mitali inched towards the door, reached for the knob.

Suddenly two thin arms jutted out from the mirror. Two gnarled hands, like the branches of a thorn bush, gripped Kelly around the neck.

The hands scratched and tore like a hawk's deadly talons. Then they grabbed. And they pulled.

8

TUG OF WAR

The bathroom door flew open, slammed shut. Mitali fled. Scared to death, she left them alone. Gone, gone.

Liam stood frozen, his shoulder blades pressed hard against the wall, as the creature's bare, grey arms – like pale, uncoiled snakes that had never seen the sun – wrapped around Kelly's throat and dragged her towards the mirror.

Bloody Mary's face howled in triumph,

'YOU DARE PLAY GAMES WITH ME, FOOLISH GIRL? NOW YOU SHALL FREE ME, WICKED ONE. TAKE MY PLACE BEHIND THE MIRROR — HERE IN THE SHADOW REALM OF THE UNDEAD!'

Kelly turned to Liam, her eyes desperate, pleading. She choked out the words, 'Help. Me.'

At once, Liam seemed to wake. He leaped to his sister, tightened his arms around Kelly's waist. Liam pulled in one direction. The creature, Bloody Mary, pulled even harder. They were locked in a tug of war.

Liam fought till his muscles ached. His feet slid on the smooth surface of the floor. He pulled with all his strength, but he felt his grip weakening. Liam was losing hold. Kelly was now inches from the mirror, wild-eyed, frantic.

I'm losing her, Liam thought.

'Dad!' Liam cried. And desperately, foolishly, 'Mom!'

His eyes seized upon a soap dish on the counter. He strained for it, grabbed it, and hurled the dish into the mirror.

A cry of shock and **CRASH!** The mirror spiderwebbed into a hundred shards of jagged glass. The creature lunged once more for Kelly, snatched at her necklace, ripped it from her throat. Bloody Mary pulled her prize back behind the shattered glass.

And it was over.

Liam flipped on the light. Kelly hugged him, and he held her tight. Kelly brought a hand to her neck, her chest. 'Mom's ring,' she said, panic rising in her voice. 'Liam! That *thing* . . . took Mom's ring!'

'Your face,' Liam said. Three red lines were slashed across Kelly's face.

The next sounds they heard were Mr Finn's heavy boots charging up the stairs. Mitali must have found him. 'What's going on up there?!' he yelled.

They'd have some explaining to do.

FIRE, FIRE,
BURNING BRIGHT

Kelly's fever started that night. 'You're burning up,' Mr Finn said. He pressed a wet washcloth against her forehead. A phone call was made, and Mitali's parents arrived to pick up their terrified daughter. There would be no sleepovers in the new house.

On the first day of her strange illness, Kelly slept fitfully. She tossed and turned and cried out, 'No, no, no!' When awake,

she worked feverishly, her black hair tangled and wet with perspiration. She didn't want to eat, refused to talk. Instead, from her bed, she drew picture after picture – with felt-tip pens, pencils, watercolours, charcoal. Kelly drew quickly, without thought or reflection, as if the images burned directly from her hand.

She had never been much of an artist. Not before. But now it was the only thing Kelly cared to do.

She drew and drew.

An artist possessed.

Maybe it was her way of dealing with what happened. The scare from Bloody Mary in the mirror, the terror of the stolen ring. Kelly consoled herself with the calm and quiet of making pictures. Glassy-eyed, she moved a dull pencil across a thick white page.

Kelly turned slowly from where she sat in her bed, pillows propped behind her, careful not to disturb the felt-tip pens and papers on the blanket. Her eyes fell on the walls of her room, admiring the artwork. A strange, distant smile fell across her face. Each wall was covered with the drawings she had taped there. Dozens of them.

Of every size and shape.

Each drawing was different, yet the same.

Each drawing was a house.

This very house.

With two eyes and a nose.

And it was on fire.

THE WAR WITHIN
THE WALLS

The noises grew more fierce at night. Late in the midnight dark, after everyone else had gone to sleep, Liam lay awake, too frightened to move. His eyes glued to the walls.

Was there a new crack there? A fragile, jagged line that ran down that wall — a crack that wasn't there yesterday?

Was something trying to claw through?

The sounds were high-pitched animal

cries, sharp, shrill shrieks and unearthly moans. A witchy wailing. Doolin climbed up in Liam's bed, hackles raised, shivering.

'Shhh,' Liam whispered. 'Easy, girl.' He held the dog and felt comforted by her animal warmth.

Dad doesn't hear it, Liam thought. Most nights his father slept downstairs, crashed out on the sofa, the TV droning on and on. Mr Finn didn't realize there was a war going on within the walls, a contending of opposites, like two wild animals locked in deadly battle. A clash of clawed eyes, angry cries, and torn skin.

I'll tell him tomorrow, Liam promised himself. *If tomorrow comes.*

He had his doubts.

Finally, Liam could not stand it any longer. He climbed out of bed, knocked on Kelly's door. 'It's me,' he whispered.

He opened it a crack. Kelly leaned up on one elbow, waved him inside.

'You hear it too?' she asked.

Yes, Liam nodded.

Kelly's eyes were unfocused, jittery. Liam felt her forehead. It was hot, moist. Her fingers twitched.

'Could it be animals?' she asked. 'Raccoons or rats in the walls?'

Liam looked away. He didn't think it was animals.

'Do you think it's her?' he asked.

'Bloody Mary?'

A bloodcurdling cry came from behind the wall. The squeal of an eagle's attack. Kelly instinctively reached for her neck, feeling for something that was not there.

'It sounds like she's fighting something . . . or someone,' Liam said.

Kelly hung her head. 'She took it.'

'Mom's ring,' Liam remembered. 'You can get another, Kell – Mom had all kinds of jewellery.'

Kelly shook her head. 'You don't understand, Liam. That ring was special to Mom. As long as I had it, I felt safe. Like Mom was with me, my guardian angel. Always looking out for us.'

Liam leaned close against his sister, looked into her misty eyes.

'And now she's gone,' Kelly said. 'She's gone forever.'

The fierce war within the walls died down. The room filled with silence, like air entering a balloon. And for the first time in years, Kelly and Liam shared the same bed, huddled close for protection.

Neither one slept.

THE STORY
OF MARY

The next morning, they discovered that Doolin was gone.

'What do you mean, gone?' Mr Finn asked. He gulped down a glass of orange juice while filling a Thermos with coffee.

'I've looked everywhere,' Liam said.

'You think she got out?'

'Dad,' Liam barked, frustrated. 'I'm telling you she's not here. It's like she ran away or . . .'

Or something.

Could something have hurt Doolin? Liam's mind turned to Bloody Mary and the mirror. Could she have taken his dog?

'We have to find her. I'm afraid something bad's happened.'

Mr Finn banged the counter with the edge of his palm. CRACK. He was a strong man and it was a loud noise. 'Look, Liam, I don't have time for this now,' he said. There was anger and frustration in his voice. 'I'm sorry, but I'm late for work already.'

'But, Dad!'

Mr Finn ran two tense hands through his hair, elbows raised to eye level. 'Liam, please. Listen to me. I am having a hard, hard time at the new job. It's not what I thought it would be. Not at all. The hours, the conditions, my boss . . .' His voice trailed off. 'I cannot be late for work, Liam. It's not an option, not with these people.'

Liam scowled at his father. He didn't care.

'Doolin is a smart old dog,' Mr Finn said, trying to make it right. 'If she got out, I'm sure she's nosing around in the woods out back. Maybe she caught a scent and followed it. She'll come back, I promise. It'll be OK.'

'You can't promise anything,' Liam said to his father, as cold and as hard as he could make the words sound. 'Nothing is OK. I hate this house, and I hate you!' he shouted, and bounded up the stairs.

The front door slammed. The car revved up, pulled out of the driveway, and raced away, hurling small stones from the back tyres.

Kelly came to him then. She entered his room, sat on the edge of his bed, and placed her hand on his back. 'We'll find Doolin,' she said. 'I feel better now. We'll make posters and put them up on all the telephone poles. We'll knock on doors. We'll find her.'

Liam steadied his breath. Wiped his face with the cuff of a sleeve. 'OK,' he said into the pillow. 'Thanks.'

A heavyset, Hispanic-looking boy on a bicycle pedalled up as they stapled the hand-made flyer to a pole. He wore jeans and an oversized white T-shirt. One foot on the ground, the other remaining on a pedal, he made a show of reading the poster.

He seemed about Kelly's age, maybe older. 'That your dog?'

'She went missing last night,' Kelly answered.

The boy had dark eyes, thick brows, and

MISSING
PLEASE HELP

DOOLIN

506-266-3674

soft cheeks. He pulled a piece of liquorice from his back pocket and bit off half of it. He chewed thoughtfully.

'You the guys who moved into the old Cropsey house?'

Liam shrugged.

'Nineteen Tudor Road.' Kelly pointed down the road. 'The big grey one.'

The boy's eyes narrowed. 'Seen anything weird?'

Kelly drew closer to Liam. She asked the boy what he meant.

And so the boy said that it was a ghost house, famous all around these parts. 'Ask anybody,' he said, and shoved the rest of the liquorice into his mouth.

'I'm Marco Torres,' he said.

Liam and Kelly told him their names.

'They say there used to be a lady who lived there, long ago,' Marco said. He leaned

in, spoke softly. 'They say she was crazy, *dama loca* they called her. She wandered these streets, lost as a little girl, howling at the moon. Anyway, one night, she got killed by a hit-and-run driver – didn't even slow down to see if she was OK. Which she wasn't, on account of she was dead.'

'What was her name?' Kelly asked.

'Bloody Mary, that's all I know,' Marco said. 'On account of all the blood. Ever since, lots of different people have tried living in that house. But nobody's ever stayed for long.'

'Why not?' Liam asked.

Marco laughed. 'By the looks on your faces, you already know the answer. Good luck, fellas. You're gonna need it.'

He saluted them with a grin, pushed off with one foot, rose up stylishly on a pedal, and was gone. Pretty smooth for a big guy.

THE LETTERS
ON THE FRIDGE

That night, the Finns sat together at the kitchen table.

Doolin had not returned. There were no phone calls, no sightings on the streets. She had simply vanished, and Liam's heart ached. Doolin was the family dog, true, but Liam had always thought of her as *his* dog, for he had loved her best.

When Mr Finn got home, he did everything

he could. Made phone calls to animal hospitals and vets, even to the police. He hauled the kids into the car and they drove the streets in slow circles, shouting out, over and over, 'Doolin, Doolin! Here, girl. Come!'

But she did not come.

Home again, it all came out. Liam talked, and Kelly talked, and Mr Finn listened. They told him everything. He nodded, and asked questions – but mostly he listened.

He finally leaned back in his chair. Ran a hand through his hair. 'I don't know, kids,' he finally said. 'I can see that you're upset. But it sounds to me like maybe your imaginations got the best of you. You have to admit that it's possible—'

A sharp, angry scraping noise interrupted Mr Finn in mid-sentence.

They turned to locate the source of the

piercing sound. It came from the refrigerator door. Mr Finn had senselessly, and uselessly, brought from the old house a bucket of magnetic letters. They came in bright colours – red, yellow, green, and blue. The kids used to play with them all the time, writing words: C-A-T and M-O-M and F-O-O-D. But no one used them any more. The letters were arrayed in a confused jumble on the door. An outgrown toy.

But now the letters slid and moved across the white surface of the refrigerator. Up and down, diagonal and across.

Nothing touched them. The letters . . . just . . . moved.

'It's a message,' Liam said.

'GET OUT NOW,' Kelly read.

They looked at one another, unsure of what to do.

More letters continued to slide into place.

Beneath the first message, it read:

LOVE

MOM

Loud, urgent barking erupted from the front lawn. They raced to the front door, opened it wide. 'Doolin!' cried Liam. 'You're back!'

The dog barked and barked from the middle of the lawn, turned to run, scampered back, and then barked more urgently. She would not come into the house.

So Liam walked out on to the cool night grass to soothe the distressed animal. Kelly and Mr Finn came with him, all murmuring gentle noises. 'What's the matter, girl? Did you miss us? What's wrong?'

KA-BOOM!

A violent blast roared from the basement. It shook the walls and blew out the windows.

The house filled with smoke and danced with roiling flames. In seconds, it was all ablaze. They had got out just in time.

WHAT THEY FOUND

The fire raged for hours, its wild flames licking at the sky like the tongues of a thousand angry snakes. For the volunteer firefighters, there was not much to be done — dry, old timber burns quick. Instead they worked to control the damage, laying down a steady rain of foam along the borders of the house to keep the fire from spreading.

Wind was the enemy now, for wind could stoke the flames ever higher, but the night

was strangely calm. Not even a breeze.

The Finns stood huddled close together, always in contact, a hand on a shoulder, an elbow near a rib, all touching, connected. Mr Ed Finn and his two children, Kelly and Liam. A nice little family, and Doolin at their feet, licking her paws.

At one point, the old house collapsed in on itself with a **WHOOSH** and a thunderous crash, the great roof caving in, shooting bright embers into the sky. It sounded, to Liam's ears, as if the house gave one final cry, then a fading whimper, and then, at last, died.

'All my clothes,' Kelly lamented. 'Our stuff.'

'I know,' Mr Finn said. 'But we have great insurance, Kell. Mom always insisted on that. We'll get money to replace most of the things we lost. We can build a new house.'

'Here?' Liam asked.

Mr Finn looked into the eyes of his two children. 'No, I don't think so. My job's not working out so hot. I hate it, to be honest with you.' He laughed, relieved to say it out loud. 'I don't think this place was ever right for us. What about you guys?'

'I want to go back to Hopeville,' Kelly said.

'Me too,' Liam agreed.

Mr Finn glanced at the sickle moon above and sighed. 'I guess we never should have left.'

mm

In the morning, they went back to see the remains of the house one last time. There was almost nothing there. Just a heap of ash, cold and in a hundred shades of grey. After a long moment, Kelly stepped forward.

She pointed. 'What's that?'

Something sparkled in the sunlight. Then Kelly ran – kicking up small clouds of dust and ash with each step. Liam followed close behind.

Kelly came to the glimmering thing. She bent to pick it up.

'I don't believe it,' Kelly murmured, her voice full of wonder. 'Mama's ring.'

Their mother's ring glistened in the sun, still brilliant and silver, polished and bright. It was untroubled by the fire. The ring appeared to be, in fact, brand new.

Kelly smiled at Liam and her father. She held the ring up high in her palm, as if making a gift of it to the heavens, and closed her fingers, tight.

SUCH IS LIFE WHEN YOU'RE FOOLING WITH THE UNDEAD. IT'S A FRIGHT.

ASHES TO ASHES, DUST TO DUST. BUT DON'T THINK THIS IS THE END OF OUR FRIEND BLOODY MARY. SHE'S A HARD LADY TO KEEP DOWN, BECAUSE MARY'S GOT A WAY OF RISING FROM THE ASHES. EVEN NOW, SHE WAITS BENEATH FLOORBOARDS . . . IN COOL BASEMENTS . . . BEHIND BATHROOM MIRRORS.

MAYBE IN A HOME NEAR YOU.

GIVE IT A TRY SOME DARK AND LONELY NIGHT. MARY WON'T BITE (SHE SCRATCHES). FLIP OFF THE LIGHTS, TURN THIRTEEN TIMES, WHISPERING IN AN EVER-LOUDER VOICE, 'BLOODY MARY, BLOODY MARY, BLOODY MARY.'

YOU NEVER KNOW WHO MIGHT SHOW UP.

LOOKING FOR MORE
THRILLS AND CHILLS?

DON'T MISS THE SECOND

SCARY TALES
BOOK . . .

JAMES PRELLER

SCARY TALES

I SCREAM, YOU SCREAM!

Illustrated by IACOPO BRUNO

ENTER THE WORLD OF SAMANTHA CARVER, AN ORDINARY KID WHO LOVES AMUSEMENT PARKS, THE SMELL OF POPCORN, AND THE JOYFUL TERROR OF A HEART-POUNDING RIDE.

SAM'S GOT A TICKET IN HER POCKET FOR A VERY SPECIAL RIDE. SOON, THIS TICKET, RIPPED IN HALF, WILL SIGNAL THE BEGINNING OF A MOST UNUSUAL ADVENTURE — AND LEAVE SAM, ALONG WITH A BOY NAMED ANDY, SCREAMING FOR THEIR LIVES.

SO, COME ALONG. TAKE A SEAT. BUCKLE UP, NICE AND TIGHT. IT'S SURE TO BE A BUMPY RIDE. AND IF YOU NEED ANYTHING — ANYTHING AT ALL — JUST SCREAM.

THINGS GO VERY WRONG

Sam was harnessed into an open, two-seated vehicle. It looked like an old coal-mining car, big wheels on a primitive track. Nothing fancy about it. Sam felt a pang of disappointment. This wasn't what she'd expected.

Next to her sat the pale-faced boy. Up close, Sam noticed that his skin was flawless, perfectly smooth. He never looked Sam in the eyes. There was something else too, something stiff about his manner. He stared forward as if he was waiting for a bus.

Two workers in orange flight suits walked around, checking on the eight cars, making sure each passenger was safely strapped in.

Sam glanced around the warehouse. It was grey, almost plain. 'Is this . . . it?' she asked a bearded worker.

He laughed. 'No worries, missy. We haven't put in all the finishing touches. Grand openings are like that. This here is only a shuttle car that will carry you through a tunnel of solid rock. When you arrive at the loading zone, my colleagues will lead you into a high tower. No one can see this tower from the road, by the way, because it looks exactly like a massive oak tree.' He flashed a gold tooth. 'That's when you enter the dragon's mouth.'

He jabbed a wicker basket in Sam's direction. 'No mobiles.'

'Really?'

'Really,' the man confirmed. 'Messes with the electronics, like on aeroplanes. Besides, Mr Overstreet does not allow photography.'

Sam reluctantly placed her phone in the basket. The mobile represented Sam's connection to her parents and friends. By handing over the phone, Sam said goodbye to the outside world.

'Ready?' the man asked.

Before Sam could answer, the car lurched forward and her back pressed against the seat.

They clanked and rattled along the track. The car sloped down into an underground tunnel, lit by green floor lights.

Sam liked the fluorescent lights and the trapped feeling of the tunnel; she felt like she was being swallowed by a great beast. 'This is cool.' She smiled at the boy.

He didn't answer, just gripped the front rail of the car.

'I'm Sammy or Sam, just not Samantha. Oh, I don't care. Take your pick!' she said cheerfully. 'What's your name?'

Sam saw his lips move. But she couldn't hear a word the boy said. The explosions were too deafening.

Sam's ears rang from the noise. Startled, she tried to turn in her seat, locate the source of the blasts, but the harness was too tight. The boy tilted his head forward, hands over his ears, eyes closed. Clouds of smoke and grit began to fill the tunnel. He coughed softly.

Could this be the ride? Sam wondered. It didn't seem right. She pulled the top of her shirt over her mouth to keep out the smoke. Sam recalled the sky, how it had shimmered strangely just before they entered the warehouse. Her feeling of being watched from above. Then came another explosion, louder than before. A jagged crack formed on the ceiling. Large chunks of rock and granite crashed behind them.

Sam yanked fiercely at her harness, pulling an arm through and twisting herself around. She saw that they were cut off from the rest of the passenger cars. Separated by an avalanche of rock. She heard screams, muffled from behind the fallen rocks. They were the screams of frightened and desperate children, who might be injured, bleeding, buried alive.

'Something has gone wrong. This should not be happening,' the boy said. He clutched at Sam's hand. His fear charged through Sam's body like an electric current. 'Those kids back there . . .'

He dared not finish the sentence.

Sam knew he was right.

Something had gone terribly wrong.

And the car rolled on through the smoke-filled dark.

SCARY TALES

JAMES PRELLER
is an extremely experienced
author of mystery-horror
stories for children. He lives
in New York with his wife,
three kids, two cats and a
golden labradoodle
called Daisy.

IACOPO BRUNO
is a graphic artist and
illustrator who lives in Italy.

OUR BOOKS ARE FRIENDS FOR LIFE.